This Book B

Thanks for buying this book! I hope it makes you giggle!

Glossary

Beefeater - *noun;* a Royal warder of the Tower of London

Bejewelled - *verb;* to adorn or decorate with or as if with jewels

Bumfuzzle - *verb;* to fluster or confuse.

Coronation - *noun;* the ceremony or act of crowning a king or queen

Splendiferous - *adjective;* splendid; magnificent; fine.

Tizzy - *noun;* an excited, nervous or distracted state

Twiddle - *verb;* to turn, fiddle or twirl; to be occupied by trifles.

The King's Crown is a House for a Mouse

Erik Eblana

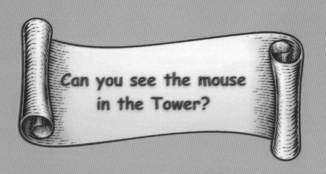

Can you see the mouse in the Tower?

In the
Tower of London,
Where the
Crown Jewels
Are shown,
A clever little mouse
Has his happy home.

The King's
Golden Crown
Is the mouse's little house.
It sparkles.
It shines.
Of which he's very proud.

He sits on a cushion
All soft and squishy,
And when he's asleep
He dreams of things cheesy.

Inside the crown
He hides all his food.
Cheese squeezed in the gold
And nuts behind the jewels.

But don't get me wrong,
He keeps his house tidy.
The gold he cleans weekly,
And the jewels
He licks shiny!

Can you see the mouse
in the Royal carriage?

Then one day,
The Beefeaters,
In their funny hats arrived,
To take the crown away
But the mouse,
Was still inside!

The little mouse
Peeped out in wonder,
As they took the crown
Through the streets of London,
On a carriage of gold,
Pulled by horses.
The mouse in the crown
Looking quite gorgeous.

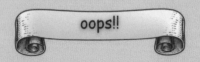
oops!!

Along the streets,
The cheering crowds,
Gathered to see,
The King's gold crown.
The mouse inside was so amused.
He smiled, he waved,
He twerked, he whooped!
And giggled when,
A horse had pooped!

Soon the carriage,
Passed Buckingham Palace.
Where a band played cheery
Tunes and ballads.
Soldiers stood guard,
In black furry hats,
And saluted the crown,
As it rolled past.
The cute little mouse,
Sang Along,
To 'Rule, Britannia!'
His favorite song.

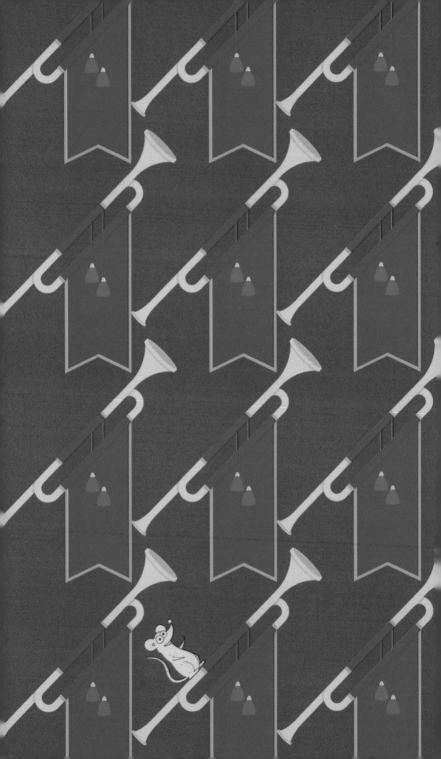

The carriage arrived
At Westminster Abbey,
To a fanfare of trumpets,
And people so happy.
The crown, on the cushion,
Was taken inside,
With the mouse in the crown,
Trying to hide.
He hummed to himself,
Not to get flustered.
So calmly sat down,
And thought of,
Cheese custard.

How many trumpets
can you see?

CALM DOWN AND STOP BEING SO FUSSY

King Charles

The Beefeaters handed,
The King his crown,
And the Bishop looked down,
With a curious frown.
'A mouse!', He yelled.
He was all in a tizzy.
But the King said,
'Calm Down
And
Stop Being
So Fussy!'.
For the little mouse,
Was frozen in fear.
When he saw the King,
Standing there,
All he could do, was,
Sit and stare.

'He's just a mouse',
Said the King with a laugh.
'But he is in my crown
And that's awfully daft.'
Just then, the mouse
Squeaked back to him,
'Your Majesty, this crown's my home,
And here you'll see, the food I've stored.'
He pointed to cheese,
Squished in the gold
And a peanut,
Behind an emerald.

The King smiled,
And then the Bishop said,
'My dear little mouse,
This may be your house
And the cushion your comfortable bed.
But it is the Kings crown,
And I need it, now,
To place on His Majesty's head!'
'That may be so,
But where shall I go,
And what of my food',
The mouse said.

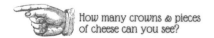 How many crowns & pieces
of cheese can you see?

DON'T WORRY STAY CALM

King Charles

'Don't worry, stay calm',
Said the King to the mouse,
'Let us agree,
That the crown is your house
But also, my crown for the day,
And when we're all done,
You can return,
With the crown, to the Tower today'.

The mouse squeaked agreement.
He bowed to the King,
Who then bowed back to the mouse.
The Bishop clapped his hands,
And the Coronation began
As everyone eyed
The Crown.

All through the Abbey,
The crowd was hushed.
Nothing stirred,
Not even the mouse.
As the bishop lifted
The golden crown,
And mumbled,
Some magical words:
'Bumfuzzle. Twiddle toot.'
The mouse was sure he said,
As he sat amazed,
To see his house,
Plonked down,
On His Majesty's head.

 How many Beefeaters can you count?

The crowd in the Abbey,
Went totally batty,
With everyone dancing around.
From Brighton to Balfour,
All would remember,
The day King Charles was crowned:
With a golden crown,
Squished with cheese,
And bejeweled with
A selection of nuts.
That splendiferous day,
The King was crowned,
With a crown,
That's a house,
For a
Mouse.

The End

Printed in Great Britain
by Amazon

21731876R00016